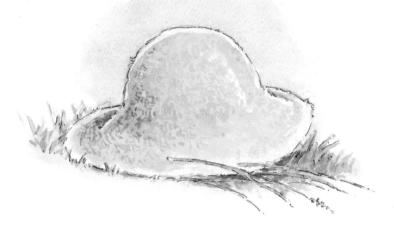

Sitting on the Farm

Written by Bob King

Illustrated by Bill Slavin

KIDS CAN PRESS LTD.
Toronto

Kids Can Press Ltd. acknowledges with appreciation the assistance of the Canada Council and the Ontario Arts Council in the production of this book.

CANADIAN CATALOGUING IN PUBLICATION DATA

King, Bob
      Sitting on the farm

ISBN 1-55074-037-7 (bound)   1-55074-149-7 (pbk.)

I. Slavin, Bill.   II. Title.

PS8571.I54S5   1991   jC813'.54   C91-093331-6
PZ7.K55Si   1991

Kids Can Press Ltd.
29 Birch Avenue
Toronto, Ontario, Canada
M4V 1E2

Designed by N.R. Jackson
Typeset by Cybergraphics Co. Inc.
Printed and bound in Hong Kong

PA 93 0 9 8 7 6 5 4 3 2 1

To my son, Kris

B.K.

For my parents, Bill and Dorothy

B.S.

Sitting on the farm, happy as can be,
I had a little bug on my knee.
I said, "Hey, Bug, get off my knee."
Well, that old bug said, "No siree!"
So I picked up the telephone,
I called my friend the frog at home.
I asked if she would like some lunch,
The frog came over and . . .

MUNCH!
MUNCH!
MUNCH!

Sitting on the farm, happy as can be,
Now I had a frog on my knee.
I said, "Hey, Frog, get off my knee."
Well, that old frog said, "No siree!"
So I picked up the telephone,
I called my friend the snake at home.
I asked if he would like some lunch,
The snake came over and . . .

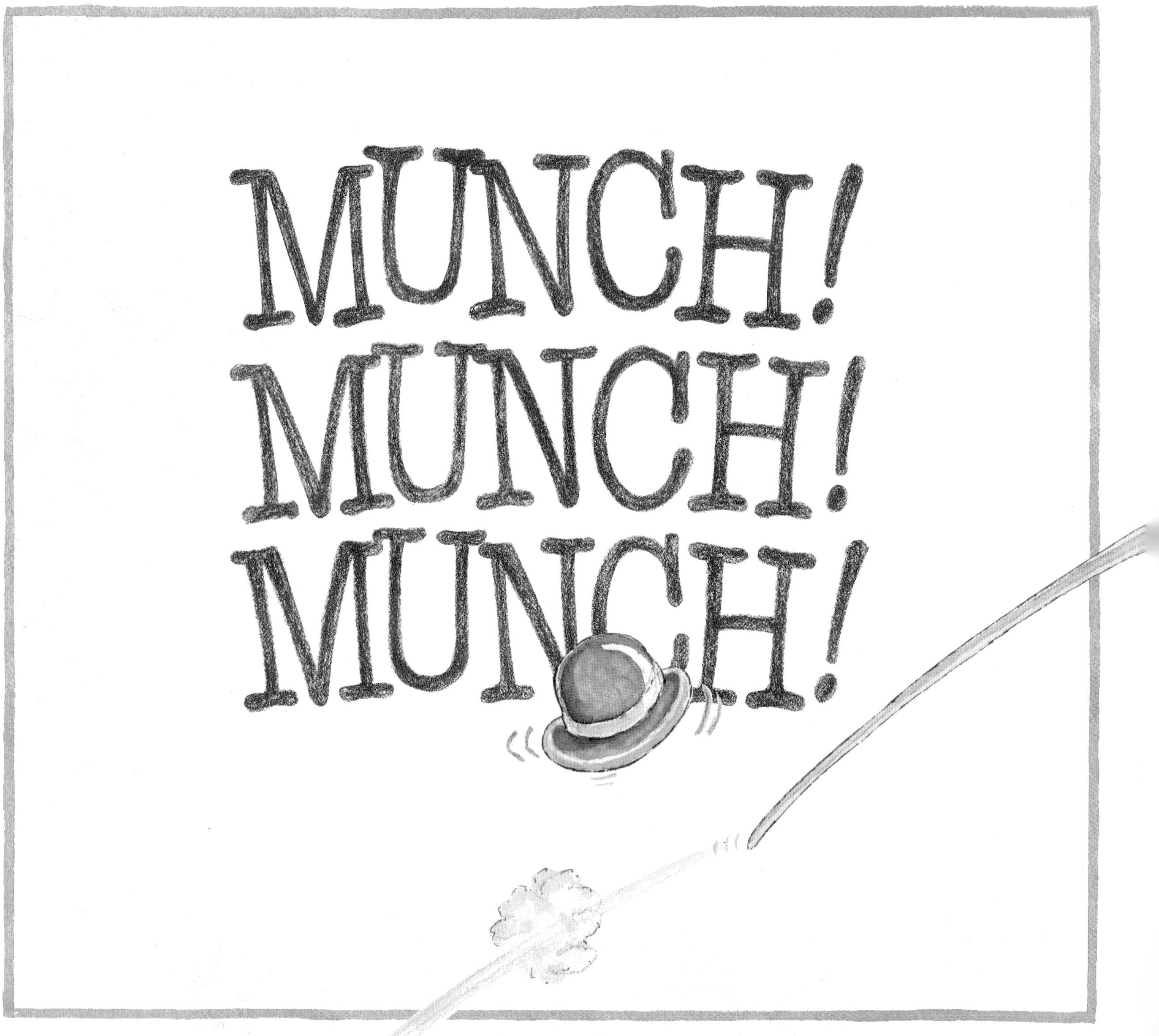
MUNCH!
MUNCH!
MUNCH!

Sitting on the farm, happy as can be,
Now I had a snake on my knee.
I said, "Hey, Snake, get off my knee."
Well, that old snake said, "No siree!"
So I picked up the telephone,
I called my friend the rat at home.
I asked if he would like some lunch,
The rat came over and . . .

MUNCH!
MUNCH!
MUNCH!

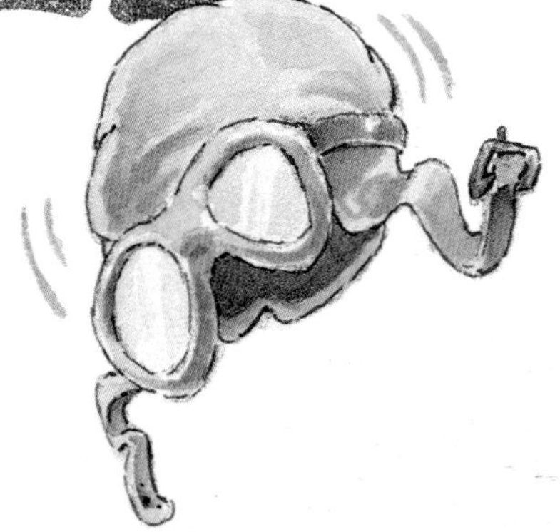

Sitting on the farm, happy as can be,
Now I had a rat on my knee.
I said, "Hey, Rat, get off my knee."
Well, that old rat said, "No siree!"
So I picked up the telephone,
I called my friend the cat at home.
I asked if she would like some lunch,
The cat came over and . . .

MUNCH! MUNCH! MUNCH!

Sitting on the farm, happy as can be,
Now I had a cat on my knee.
I said, "Hey, Cat, get off my knee."
Well, that old cat just looked at me.
So I picked up the telephone,
I called my friend the dog at home.
I asked if he would like some lunch,
The dog came over and . . .

Sitting on the farm, happy as can be,
Now I had a dog on my knee.
I said, "Hey, Dog, get off my knee."
Well, that old dog said, "No siree!"
So I picked up the telephone,
I called my friend the bear at home.
I asked if she would like some lunch,
The bear came over and . . .

MUNCH!
MUNCH!
MUNCH!

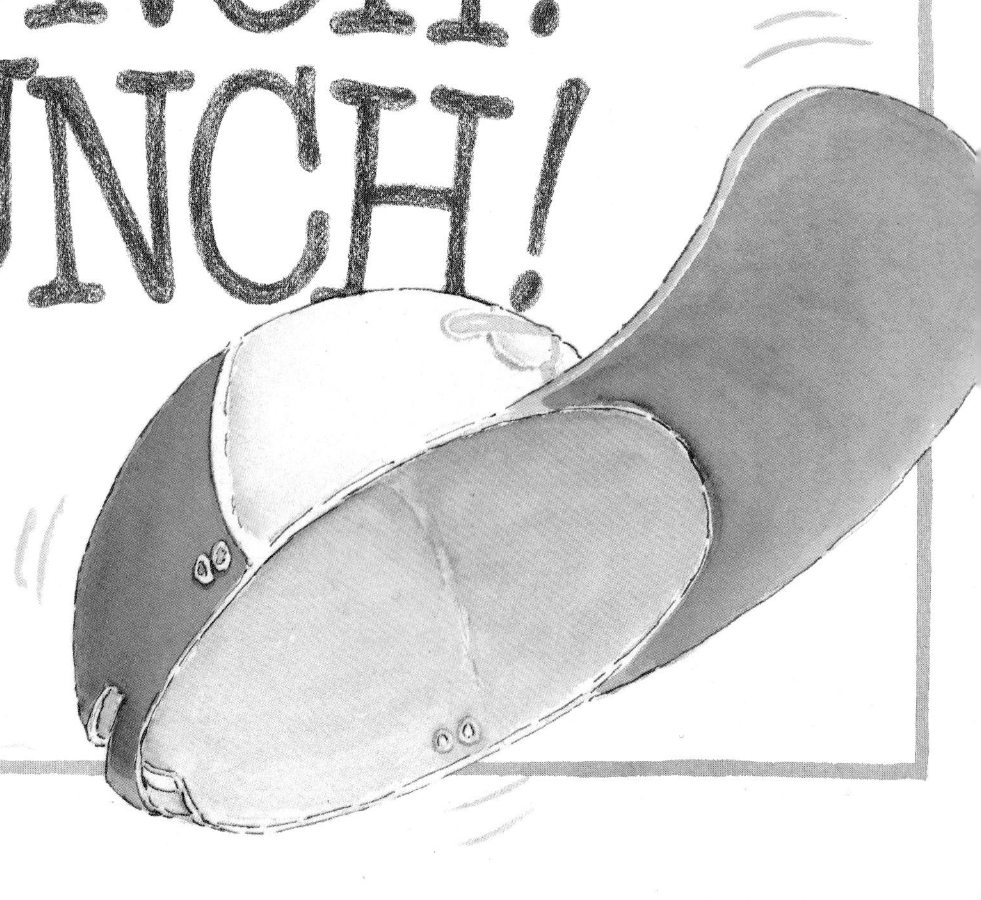

Sitting on the farm, happy as can be,
Now I had a bear on my knee.
I said, "Hey, Bear, get off my knee."
Well, that old bear said, "No siree!"
So I picked up the telephone,
I called my friend the —

Won't somebody please help me,
Get this bear off my knee . . .

Sitting on the Farm

Sitting on the farm, happy as can be, I had a little bug

on my knee. I said, "Hey, Bug, get off my knee." Well, that old bug said,

"No siree!" So I picked up the telephone, I called my friend the

frog at home. I asked if she would like some lunch, The frog came over and . . .

MUNCH! MUNCH! MUNCH!